The Fun Day Fairies

For Thea Rose Killacky Wheeler,
with lots of love

Special thanks to
Sue Mongredien

ORCHARD BOOKS
338 Euston Road, London NW1 3BH
Orchard Books Australia
Level 17/207 Kent Street, Sydney, NSW 2000
A Paperback Original

First published in Great Britain in 2006

© 2009 Rainbow Magic Limited.
A HIT Entertainment company. Rainbow Magic
is a trademark of Rainbow Magic Limited.
Reg. U.S. Pat. & Tm. Off. And other countries.

HiT entertainment

Illustrations © Georgie Ripper 2006

A CIP catalogue record for this book is available
from the British Library.

ISBN 978 1 84616 191 9
7 9 10 8 6

Printed in Great Britain

Orchard Books is a division of Hachette Children's Books,
an Hachette UK company

www.hachette.co.uk

Thea
the Thursday Fairy

by Daisy Meadows

illustrated by Georgie Ripper

ORCHARD BOOKS

www.rainbowmagic.co.uk

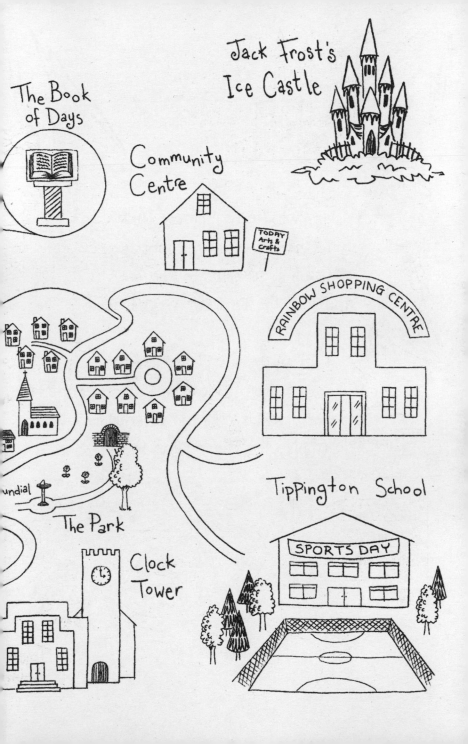

Icy wind now fiercely blow!
To the Time Tower I must go.
Goblin servants follow me
And steal the Fun Day Flags I need.

I know there will be no fun,
For fairies or humans once the flags are gone.
So, storm winds, take me where I say.
My plan for chaos starts today!

Contents

Spectacular Seahorses

"A tropical reef, a sunken galleon, sea otters, seahorses, giant Japanese spider crabs, reef sharks... Wow!" Rachel Walker looked up from the colourful leaflet she was holding and grinned at her friend Kirsty Tate. "We're going to have a brilliant time here!"

The two girls had come to Morristown
Aquarium for the day with Rachel's
parents. Kirsty was spending the
half-term week with Rachel and they
had been having a very exciting time.
A very magical time too!

"We'll meet you back here at four
o'clock," Mrs Walker said, as they all
strolled into the entrance lobby.
"Have fun!"

"We will," Rachel said cheerfully, but then she gazed at some of the other people nearby. "Although it doesn't look as if anyone else is having fun," she whispered to Kirsty.

Kirsty looked around. Rachel was right. There were plenty of visitors at the aquarium but they didn't seem to be enjoying themselves.

"I don't even like fish," they heard one boy mutter. "Why did we have to come here?"

Rachel and Kirsty gave each other a knowing look as Rachel's parents wandered off to look at the first exhibit.

They knew exactly why the atmosphere seemed so flat. It was because the Thursday Fun Day Flag was missing!

Rachel and Kirsty were friends with the fairies, and had been busy helping them all week. Nasty Jack Frost had stolen the seven Fun Day Flags from the Time Tower in Fairyland, and without them, the Fun Day Fairies couldn't spread their special magic around the human world. Jack Frost had taken the flags back to his castle, but had soon decided that this was a mistake: his goblin servants had had so much fun, they had stopped doing any work! In a rage, Jack Frost had hurled the flags into the human world, and now Rachel and Kirsty were helping the fairies to find them.

But, unknown to their master, the sneaky goblins were trying to try to get the flags back, too!

Kirsty turned to Rachel. "We've just got to find that Thursday flag before the goblins do," she whispered. "We really need to cheer everybody up in here."

"Definitely," Rachel agreed. "But you know what the fairies say: we have to let the magic find us. So why don't we have a look at some of the exhibits?" She opened up the map inside her leaflet, and Kirsty leaned over for a closer look.

"Ooh, seahorses, I love those,"
Kirsty said, spotting a picture of some.
"Let's head for the tropical reef
section, then," Rachel suggested.
"That's where all the seahorses are."
The girls walked along a corridor
filled with brightly lit fish
tanks. They stopped to
see the large orange
and purple flame
angel fish gliding
along elegantly, the
yellow and white
copperband butterfly
fish darting to
and fro, and the
cheerful-looking
orange and white clown
fish swimming happily about.

"And here are the seahorses!"
Rachel said, as they drew level with
the next tank.

Kirsty and Rachel both gazed through
the glass to watch the beautiful red
and yellow creatures bobbing about
vertically like tiny watery dragons.
There were rocks and coral at the
bottom of their tanks, and long green
weeds, which the seahorses seemed
to like hiding in.

"Wow!" Kirsty exclaimed. "That one just changed colour from yellow to black!"

"Amazing!" Rachel commented, studying the information board. "Oh yes, it says here that they can turn from black or grey to yellow or red. How cool!"

"Oh, and look – baby seahorses!" Kirsty cooed. "They are so adorable. Can you see them?"

Suddenly, Kirsty heard a friendly voice behind her say, "Ahh, but did you know that with seahorses it's the dad who has the babies, not the mum?"

The girls turned to see a member of staff smiling at them.

"Really?" Rachel asked, interested. "I didn't know that."

The aquarium guide started telling the girls how the female seahorses fought over the male seahorses with the biggest bellies! "That's where the males have their breeding pouch," he explained. "So the bigger the belly, the better the father – but that only counts for seahorses!"

Rachel laughed, and Kirsty nodded, but Rachel could see that her friend was rather distracted. She was staring into the tank, and it was only when the guide strolled away again that Kirsty turned to Rachel, her eyes shining.

"Look who I've just seen!" she hissed, pointing at the glass.

Rachel followed the line of Kirsty's finger and a smile lit up her face. Right at the back of the tank, riding a yellow seahorse with blue spots, sat a tiny smiling fairy, waving at the girls!

Underwater Fairy

"It's Thea the Thursday Fairy!" Rachel said, her voice hushed with excitement. "Hello again, Thea!" The girls had met all seven of the Fun Day Fairies when they'd been magically whisked to Fairyland on Monday.

Thea guided her seahorse towards the girls with a grin. She had long golden

hair, and wore a long-sleeved lilac
dress with a white belt. A beautiful
amethyst pendant necklace sparkled
at her throat.

Thea's seahorse floated right up to
the glass and Thea started to say
something to the girls, pointing behind
them. Unfortunately, the tank's glass
was so thick, Rachel and Kirsty
couldn't hear what she was saying.

"What's she pointing at?" Kirsty wondered aloud, turning to see. "Ah! Do you think she means we're to meet her over there?"

Rachel looked where Kirsty was indicating and saw a large seahorse sculpture in the corner of the room near a tank of silver eels. She turned back to the glass, and saw that Thea was nodding enthusiastically at them.

"I think so," Rachel said, smiling. "Okay, Thea, we'll see you there in a minute!"

The two girls went over to the
sculpture at once, both feeling excited
that another fairy
adventure was
about to begin.
"I'm looking
forward to hearing
the next poem from
the Book of Days,"
Kirsty said in a low voice.

"Me, too," Rachel said. "Hopefully it
will give us a clue to where the missing
flag is. It might even be in one of
the tanks!"

The girls grinned at one another. The
Book of Days was looked after by
Francis, Fairyland's Royal Time Guard,
and he used it to tell which day it was
and which flag he should run up the

flagpole every morning. Ever since the flags had been stolen, though, a new riddle had magically appeared in the book each day. So far, the riddles had helped Rachel, Kirsty and the fairies find three of the missing Fun Day Flags.

"Looking for the flags is like the best kind of treasure hunt," Kirsty said happily. "It's—"

But before Kirsty could finish her sentence, Rachel nudged her friend. "I've just seen a goblin!" she said. "Look – he's snorkelling with those eels!"

Kirsty and Rachel hid behind the
sculpture so that the goblin wouldn't
notice them. He was swimming
along at the top of the tank, wearing
a snorkel mask and big flippers on
his feet. Luckily, there was nobody
else in the room to notice him.

"He must think the Thursday flag is
in there," Kirsty said in a low voice.
"Can you see it anywhere, Rachel?"

The two friends peered cautiously
into the tank, looking all around for
a sparkly fairy flag, but there was no
sign of it.

Just then, the air beside the sculpture shimmered, and Thea appeared in a flurry of pink sparkles.

"Hello again," Rachel said. Then she gazed curiously at the smiling fairy. "I thought you'd be wet after your swim, but you're completely dry!" she exclaimed.

"And you could breathe underwater, without a bubble helmet!" Kirsty added. "When we went underwater with Summer the Holiday Fairy, we had to use bubbles. How come you didn't need one?"

Thea winked and twirled her wand between her fingers. "Fairy magic is wonderful stuff," she laughed.

"It's lucky you're here," Rachel went on, "because look who's in this eel tank!"

Thea turned and saw the swimming goblin, but she didn't seem terribly alarmed. "Don't worry," she assured the girls, "he won't find anything in there. I've already checked all the tanks in this area and the Thursday Fun Flag definitely isn't in any of them."

"But it is in the aquarium?" Kirsty asked eagerly.

"Yes," Thea said, "but we're going to have to be really careful, because we're not the only ones looking for it. There are goblins all over the place!"

Goblins Galore!

Rachel and Kirsty looked around
nervously. They certainly didn't want
any lurking goblins to know that
they, too, were searching for the
Thursday Fun Flag.

Once she was quite sure that
they weren't going to be overheard,
Rachel turned back to Thea.

"Has a new poem appeared in the Book of Days?" she asked.

Thea nodded. "Francis told me it this morning," she replied. "And this is how it goes." The fairy lowered her voice and recited:

"*Seahorses, turtles and sharks abound*
In the aquarium, the flag will be found.
Look among all the beautiful fish;
On the back of the whale, you'll find
your wish."

"On the back of the whale…" Kirsty repeated thoughtfully. "Rachel, are there any whales in this aquarium?"

Rachel unfolded her leaflet and scanned it quickly. "There's a whale shark exhibit nearby," she announced. "The flag might be there."

"Let's go and see!" Thea said, fluttering into Kirsty's pocket.

The whale sharks' tank was in the very next room. After the small seahorse tanks, it seemed absolutely vast, stretching across one whole wall.

"Look how enormous the whale sharks are!" Rachel marvelled. "No wonder they need such a huge home."

"These two are called Griffin and Chloe, and they're eight metres long," Kirsty said, reading the sign next to the tank. "Whale sharks are the biggest fish in the ocean. They grow up to fourteen metres long!" she added with a whistle.

Rachel peered in at the majestic whale sharks as they nosed their way around their tank. They were dark grey, with yellow dots and stripes on their bodies, but neither creature had a Fun Day Flag on its back. "Maybe the flag has floated loose and sunk to the bottom of the tank," she suggested.

The three friends drew closer to the tank for a better look. There was sand at its base, with clumps of brown seaweed and piles of rocks here and there. Shoals of colourful fish darted around the whale sharks, not at all bothered by the size of their tank-mates.

"Oh!" Thea gasped suddenly, from where she was peeping out of Kirsty's pocket. "Look!"

Kirsty peered into the tank, hoping Thea had spotted her sparkly flag, but she hadn't. What she had seen were two scuba divers with masks on their

faces and oxygen canisters on their
backs, slithering along the bottom of
the tank. The divers had big green feet
and long, pointy noses.

"Oh, no!" Kirsty cried, as she
realised who they were.

"More goblins!" Rachel groaned.
"They beat us to it!"

"What have they found?" Kirsty
asked in dismay, as she watched one
of the goblin divers start pulling at
something pink that was lodged
between two rocks. He beckoned his
friend over, and he came to help,
blocking the girls' view in the process.

Both goblins tugged eagerly at their find, and Thea's face fell.

"Oh, no!" she gasped. "My flag is pink. I think they've got my Thursday Fun Flag!"

Flag Ahoy!

The girls and Thea held their breath
as the goblins heaved at the pink thing.
Finally, the rocks shifted and the first
goblin held up his hand victoriously.
But his look of triumph soon turned
sour when he realised he was
clutching a piece of pinkish seaweed
and not the Thursday flag after all.

43

His friend poked him crossly, and shook
his head, which prompted the
first goblin to throw the
piece of seaweed over his
companion's head in
a huff. It was obvious
that neither goblin
was very happy.

"Thank
goodness it was
only seaweed,"
Thea breathed
in relief.

"Look! I think
Griffin and Chloe are
coming to introduce
themselves to the goblins,"
Kirsty said, her eyes wide.
Both whale sharks seemed to have

noticed the disturbance, and were now swimming straight towards the goblins. The goblins suddenly looked up to see the huge faces of Griffin and Chloe looming in front of them. With a jump of alarm, the goblins began swimming away as fast as they could. The sharks followed, curiously. "Oh, no! The sharks aren't going to eat them, are they?" Kirsty cried anxiously.

Rachel laughed. "No," she said, pointing at the information board in front of her. "It says here that whale sharks are filter feeders, who sieve their food through their gills." She grinned. "They're not dangerous at all – their food has to be tiny to fit through their sieves. They couldn't eat the goblins even if they wanted to."

Thea couldn't help giggling at the
panicking goblins. "Something
tells me that the goblins
don't know that,"
she laughed.

"It doesn't look
as if the flag's in
there, anyway,"
Kirsty added,
smiling as the
goblins floundered
towards the top of the
tank. "Any other whales
in the guide, Rachel?"

Rachel consulted her leaflet again.
"Yes," she said. "There's a beluga
whale exhibit in the aquarium. We
have to go through the underwater
tunnel to get there. This way!"

Rachel led them out of the room and
into a huge, brightly lit tunnel, where
crowds of people were gazing all
around them. The sides and roof of the
tunnel were made of thick glass, and
the girls slowed in wonder as they saw
schools of brightly coloured fish, sting

rays and turtles swimming right over their heads. A big green turtle came up to the glass near Kirsty and seemed to give her a friendly wink. She waved and smiled at him through the tunnel wall.

"We'd better go on to find the beluga whales," she said after a little while.

She was reluctant to leave the tunnel with all its fascinating sea life, but she knew that finding the flag was more important. "We can always come back here later..."

But, just then, Rachel gasped and Kirsty looked around to see that her friend was pointing further along

the tunnel. There was a

sunken wreck of a pirate ship, with fish swimming in and out of it, and as Kirsty drew closer, she saw that the name on the side of the hull was... *The Whale!*

"This might be the whale we're looking for!" Kirsty murmured excitedly. "Well spotted!"

"Yes, and look what's on the mast," Rachel whispered joyfully. "Thea's flag!"

Kirsty and Thea gazed up at the ship's sails to see that Rachel was right. Bobbing gently in the water at the top of the mast was the Thursday Fun Flag! It was a beautiful dusty pink colour, with a large glittery sun on it.

"We've found it," Thea declared happily. "Brilliant!"

Kirsty gave Rachel a nudge. "But look who else is just about to find it as well," she hissed in dismay.

Rachel and Thea turned to see three goblins dressed as little boys trooping through the tunnel.

"Oh, no!" Thea said in an anguished whisper. "We can't let them see the flag!"

Goblin Danger

A smile suddenly lit up Kirsty's face.
"I've had an idea," she said in a low
voice. "Don't look at the ship, OK?"

Rachel nodded, and turned her
gaze upon a peculiar sand-coloured
flatfish that was rising slowly
up through the water. "OK,"
she whispered.

"I've worked it out!" Kirsty said to Rachel, in a loud voice, pretending that she hadn't noticed the goblins nearby. "I've figured out just where the Thursday Fun Flag must be!"

From the corner of her eye, Rachel saw the three goblins slow down to eavesdrop on Kirsty. She grinned and began playing along with her clever friend. "Oh, where is it?" she asked eagerly.

"Well, the poem said it was on the back of a whale, didn't it?" Kirsty went on. "And the beluga whale exhibit is at the end of this tunnel!"

The goblins immediately rushed away down the tunnel, giggling with glee and completely missing the pirate ship with its Fun Day Flag treasure.

Thea fluttered out of Kirsty's pocket smiling. "Your plan worked!" she cried happily.

Kirsty was smiling, too. "Hopefully that will keep those goblins safely out of the way, while we get the flag!"

Just then, an announcement came over the tannoy system. "We will be feeding the sea otters in five minutes," a voice said. "Please make your way to the otters' habitat now, if you would like to watch." The other visitors in the tunnel started drifting away to see the otters. "Perfect," Thea whispered, hiding behind Kirsty's hair. "Now the coast is clear for some flag-collecting!"

She waved her wand over the girls,
and a stream of pink sparkles tumbled
all over them. Rachel and Kirsty felt
themselves shrinking until they were the
same size as Thea with sparkling wings
on their backs. They were fairies again!

"Since we need to get into the tank,
I've given you some underwater
magic, too," Thea said. "You'll be
able to breathe quite easily when we're
in the water."

"How do we get in?" Rachel asked, fluttering her wings excitedly.

Thea was already flying ahead to a door marked 'Staff Only' at the end of the tunnel. "This way," she called.

Kirsty, Rachel and Thea slipped through the gap under the door. On the other side were tall ladders that stretched right up to the top of the tank, for feeding purposes, Kirsty guessed. The tank was open at the top, so they flew up and over the side.

Splash! Splash! Splash! The three friends plunged into the water, which was lovely and warm.

"I feel just like a mermaid, now that I can breathe underwater," Rachel said happily, as they swam down towards the ship. A whole school of silvery fish came over to look at them curiously. "Hello," Kirsty said in a friendly way as she passed. "We're just popping in to get something, don't worry."

"There it is," Rachel said, as they neared the ship.

Kirsty joined her and, together, the girls carefully unhooked the shimmering flag from the top of the mast. Then they swam over to Thea, towing it behind them.

"Thank you," Thea said happily. She touched her wand to the Thursday flag and it shrank down to its Fairyland size. Then she waved her wand again and a flurry of twinkling pink lights danced through the water towards the ship. Within seconds, a new flag was attached to the mast with a slightly different pink and silver design.

"We did it!" Kirsty cheered. "Let's get out of here!"

But even as she spoke, Rachel cried out in alarm, because four goblin divers had emerged from inside the shipwreck!

One of the goblins spotted the flag in Thea's hand and pointed at it indignantly. He swam quickly towards the girls, followed by his three friends.

"Quick!" called Rachel urgently, as she, Kirsty and Thea began swimming away as fast as they could. They were so tiny, though, that it wasn't long before the goblins were closing in on them. Rachel could see that in another few seconds they would be surrounded and trapped!

Turtle Power

Kirsty was swimming as fast as she could when she saw the turtle she'd waved to earlier zoom over to Thea. He seemed to be saying something.

"Thank you," Thea replied after a moment, looking relieved. "He says would we like a lift?" she told the girls.

"Yes, please!" Kirsty and Rachel chorused thankfully, scrambling quickly onto the turtle's smooth green shell, as the goblins drew closer. Thea climbed aboard, too, and the turtle immediately kicked his powerful flippers, sending them shooting through the water at great speed. Within seconds, they were clear of the goblins.

The turtle peered back over his shoulder, his kindly eyes twinkling, and Thea grinned. "He just told me he's going to take the goblins on a little tour," she explained to Kirsty and Rachel.

Rachel smiled as the space between them and the goblins widened. The turtle zoomed along on a zig-zag route around some rocks, over some bright red coral, and past a large, surprised-looking octopus.

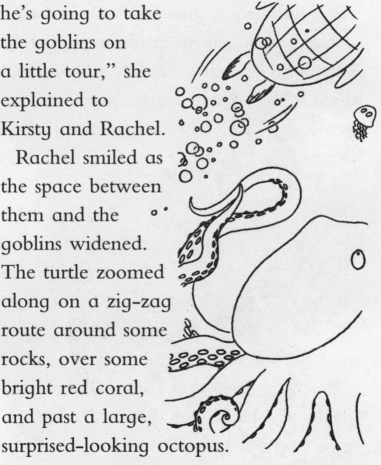

"They're still chasing us," Kirsty said, looking round to check.

But it was quite clear that the goblins were starting to tire now. One of them had given up already, and was slumped breathlessly on a rock while he watched the others. The remaining three were slowing down. They seemed to be arguing about whose fault it was that the girls and Thea had got away with the flag.

Kirsty realised that the goblins would never be able to catch up with them now and she heaved a sigh of relief.

The turtle swam smoothly up to the surface of the tank, and Kirsty, Rachel and Thea slipped off his back.

"Thank you so much," Thea said to him.

"Yes, thank you," Rachel added. "You saved us – and the Thursday flag."

"Goodbye," Kirsty said, giving the turtle a gentle pat.

He smiled at her and winked – this time there was no doubt about it! – and then he swam majestically away.

Kirsty, Rachel and Thea clambered out of the tank, shaking their heavy, wet wings behind them. Thea waved her wand and instantly all three of them were dry. Then they flew down and under the 'Staff Only' door once more.

Thea looked cautiously up and down the underwater tunnel but it was still empty, so with a wave of her wand and a blast of sparkling pink fairy dust, she turned Kirsty and Rachel back into girls.

She grinned at them both. "I'd better fly off to Fairyland to recharge my wand now," she said, "then I can put

a bit of sparkle back into Thursday
with my Fun Day Magic!" She flew
over to peep at Rachel's watch. "If you
two hurry, you might just catch the
otters being fed," she added.

"Thanks," Kirsty said. "Bye, Thea.
It was great to see you again."

Thea blew them
each a kiss, and
disappeared in
a glittering pink
blur. Rachel and
Kirsty knew that
Thea needed to give the Thursday
flag to Francis so that he could run
it up to the top of the Time Tower.
Then Thea would stand in the middle of
the clock in the Time Tower courtyard
and hold up her wand. As the sun's rays

struck the shiny pattern on the Fun Day
Flag, a stream of magical sparkles would
be channelled to Thea's wand, filling it
with powerful Fun Day Magic.

"I hope it doesn't take Thea long to
recharge her wand," Rachel said in a low
voice as they entered the otter room.
"Look at everyone in here!"

The otter room was divided in two by
a floor-to-ceiling glass wall. On one side
of the room was the sea otters' habitat,
with a stream splashing over rocks into
a large pool. A crowd of people had
gathered on the other side of the glass to
watch the otters being fed. But nobody
looked very happy about it, and even the
otters looked bored and listless. They
sniffed at the small fish that the keeper
threw them, and then ignored them

completely. Some even turned tail and went back into their sleeping quarters!

"Oh dear," Kirsty whispered. "Please hurry, Thea. Come and save the day! Nobody's having any fun."

The keeper frowned. "I don't know what's got into them," the girls heard him mutter. "Usually, these otters are right little livewires."

Just then, Rachel spotted a stream of bright pink sparkles at the back of the otters' habitat. She nudged Kirsty. "I think Thea might be back already," she smiled. "I'm sure I just spotted some fairy magic."

As she finished speaking, the otters suddenly seemed to shake themselves and wake up. They came tumbling into the water and splashed about merrily, chasing the fish that the keeper threw to them. Their sleek dark heads popped up above the water then plunged under again, as another fish dropped into their pool. Soon everyone in the crowd was smiling at their antics.

"They're adorable," Rachel said happily. "And look – everyone's having fun now."

"Thea's worked her magic all right," Kirsty laughed. "Oh, and there she is!"

The girls beamed at the tiny fairy as she peeped out from behind a rock and gave them a special wave, before disappearing once again in a pink shimmer.

Rachel glanced down at her watch. "That was a brilliant adventure," she smiled. "And best of all, we've still got some time left before we have to meet Mum and Dad."

"So we can watch the otters and see some of the other stuff," Kirsty said. She grinned at Rachel. "I've heard the beluga whale exhibit is worth checking out."

"Oh, yes," Rachel replied, laughing. "We definitely have to see that!"

Win Rainbow Magic Goodies!

There are lots of Rainbow Magic fairies, and we want to know which one is your favourite! Send us a picture of her and tell us in thirty words why she is your favourite and why you like Rainbow Magic books. Each month we will put the entries into a draw and select one winner to receive a Rainbow Magic Sparkly T-shirt and Goody Bag!

Send your entry on a postcard to Rainbow Magic Competition, Orchard Books, 338 Euston Road, London NW1 3BH. Australian readers should email: childrens.books@hachette.com.au New Zealand readers should write to Rainbow Magic Competition, 4 Whetu Place, Mairangi Bay, Auckland NZ. Don't forget to include your name and address. Only one entry per child.

Good luck!

The Fun Day Fairies

Megan, Tallulah, Willow and Thea
have got their flags back. Now
Rachel and Kirsty must help

Freya the Friday Fairy

Cooking Up a Storm

"Here's the recipe, Kirsty," Rachel
Walker said, showing the cookery book
to her best friend Kirsty Tate. "Don't
they look yummy?"

Kirsty looked at the picture and nodded.
"I love gingerbread men!" she said.

"Gran always bakes gingerbread men
for my birthday," Rachel explained. "So I
thought we could make some for her as
she's coming to tea today." She laughed
as her shaggy dog Buttons trotted into the
kitchen and looked up at the two girls
hopefully. "Buttons likes them too!"

At that moment Mrs Walker, Rachel's

mum, followed Buttons into the room. "Gran will be here soon," she said. "We'd better get started, girls. I'll find the cookie cutter. You two collect the ingredients."

"OK, Mum," Rachel agreed. "I'll get the eggs. Kirsty, could you get the flour? It's in that cupboard near the sink."

Rachel opened the fridge and Kirsty went to find the flour. Meanwhile, Mrs Walker was searching through the drawers for the cookie cutter...

Read the rest of

Freya
the Friday Fairy

to find out what magic happens next...

Have you checked out the

RAINBOW
magic®

website at:
www.rainbowmagic.co.uk